The Big Purple Wonderbook

Northamptonshire

DISCARDED

Libraries

D0715057

Sch

80 002 945 195

The Big Purple Wonderbook

by Enid Richemont
and Kelly Waldek

Evans

For Billy, Tom, Quinn and William - E.R.

First published 2008
Evans Brothers Limited
2A Portman Mansions
Chiltern St
London W1U 6NR

Text copyright © Enid Richemont 2008
© in the illustrations Evans Brothers Ltd 2008

All rights reserved. No part of this publication
may be reproduced, stored in a retrieval system
or transmitted in any form, or by any means,
electronic, mechanical, photocopying, recording
or otherwise, without the prior permission of
Evans Brothers Limited.

British Library Cataloguing in Publication Data

Richemont, Enid
  The big purple wonderbook. - (Skylarks)
  1. Children's stories
  I. Title
  823.9'14[J]

  ISBN: 978 0 237 53583 4 (HB)
  ISBN: 978 0 237 53595 7 (PB)

Printed in China by WKT Co. Ltd

Series Editor: Louise John
Design: Robert Walster
Production: Jenny Mulvanny

Northamptonshire Libraries & Information Service	
80 002 945 195	
Peters	27-Jan-2009
CF	£4.99

Contents

Chapter One   7

Chapter Two   12

Chapter Three   18

Chapter Four   23

Chapter Five   27

Chapter Six   31

Chapter Seven   35

Chapter Eight   39

Chapter One

Something inside the cardboard box called out to Tom.

"Pick me up!" it said.

Tom looked round for Mum, but she was sorting through some hats.

"Pick me up!" repeated the voice. It sounded really bossy.

Tom began turning over all the things in the box – scarves, funny handbags, bits of lace and ancient jigsaws.

The charity shop lady smiled. "Nothing much you'd want in there, love," she said.

Then Tom pulled out an old book with a purple cover.

"That took long enough," grumbled the voice.

The book had a dragon stamped on its front. It had gold edges on its pages, a silky red bookmark, and pictures that lay like precious secrets behind thin crackly paper.

"Mum," called Tom. "Can I have this, please?"

"Depends how much," said Mum, trying on a squashy velvet hat.

The charity shop lady peered over Tom's shoulder.

"The Big Purple Wonderbook," she read. "That sounds like fun." She took it for a moment. Then she gave it back.

"Five pence," she told him. "Special price. Just for you."

"OK, we'll take it," said Mum. She handed the hat to the lady. "I'll have this too."

Tom held the book close.

"Now I'm yours," whispered the voice.

"Aren't you a lucky boy?" said Mum.

Chapter Two

On the way home, Tom opened his book and lifted up the tissue on its first coloured picture.

"Hey, look at this!" he cried.

"Watch where you're going," Mum told him. "You'll fall down a hole."

Back at the house, Tom's older

brother, Edward, was prancing round the living room to music.

Mum sighed. "Turn that thing down!"

Tom showed Edward his book. "It talks," he said. "It says things."

Edward tapped Tom on the side of his head. "You're bananas!" he said.

That night, Tom showed it to Mum's new boyfriend, Mike. Mike flipped

through the pages without really
looking.

"You've got a bargain there," he said.

Tom watched TV for a while,
then he got bored and picked a fight
with Edward.

Mum got tough. "Bedtime, boys!"
she yelled.

Edward creaked around in the lower
bunk. "Show us your talking book,"
he said.

"I'm reading it," fibbed Tom.

"You can't read," teased Edward.

"Oh, yes he can," said the book.

"Did you hear that?" asked Tom.

"Of course he didn't," whispered the
book. "My voice is a secret between me
and you." It flipped open some pages.

"Try one of my stories."

"Can't," said Tom sadly. "Too many hard words."

"Don't you know the trick?" The book gave a soft, papery sigh. "Read all the easy words first, and the hard ones read themselves."

"Who are you talking to?" called out Edward.

"No one," Tom told him.

"I always knew you were bananas!" Edward sniffed.

"If you do something for me," whispered the book, "I'll tell you a story. Put your finger under my first word. Mmm," it breathed. "That feels good. Now move it along." The book wriggled. "Not too fast, boy, that tickles!"

Tom slowly moved his fingers along

the lines of words and listened to the story the book was telling.

He couldn't remember going to sleep.

But that night, he dreamed of a princess in a tower, of an island in a lake, of a snake, a ship with silver sails and a dragon that could fly.

Chapter Three

"Wake up!" Mum looked furious. "You left your light on all night, and you're going to be late for school."

Mum wasn't usually so cross.

Tom got dressed and went to the kitchen, still holding his book. "It told me a story," he said.

But Mum wasn't listening. She was looking weepy. "I've lost an earring," she said. "One of the special ones your gran gave me."

"Try looking in the bathroom," suggested Edward.

"I've looked in there," sniffed Mum. "I've looked everywhere. It's just gone." She glowered at Tom. "You're not taking that old book to school?"

"It's a talking book," joked Edward.

"Well it is," insisted Tom.

Edward went up the hill to his school, and Tom went down the hill to his.

In the wet playground, Luke came up to him.

"What's that book?" he demanded.

"It's old," said Tom. "I bought it at the charity shop yesterday."

"Let's see." Luke had a look then whistled. "It's ancient!" he said.

"I know," Tom said. "And it only cost me five pence."

Miss Taylor came over. "What's that you've brought?" she asked.

Tom showed her.

"It's got lovely gold letters," said Miss Taylor. "And super pictures."

"That's why I bought it," said Tom.

The rain went on all morning, so they had to stay inside at lunchtime. Luke had choir practice, so Tom was by himself. The book slipped from under his arm and fell into his lap. "Want a story?" it offered.

"Don't feel like one," said Tom.

The book fanned out its pages. "It's a good story. Put your finger on the line..."

It sighed. "Oh, I do like that."

Tom took his hand away. "Too many words," he argued.

"There are wishes in this one," the book said softly. "I could fix things so you could have some."

"Wishes are stupid," huffed Tom. "Wishes aren't real."

"Why not find out?"

"Ok, ok," Tom sighed. "If you insist..."

Chapter Four

Tom ran his fingers along the line and the book began its story; Once there was a fisherman...

Tom's fingers moved faster and the book began to wriggle.

"It's tickly!" it squealed. "Go slower," it ordered.

Steve, the class bully, came barging up to Tom. "What's that rubbish you've got there?" he demanded.

"It's a book," muttered Tom. "Can't you see?"

Steve pushed the book hard into Tom's face.

"Ow!" yelled Tom. "I hate you, Steve Morris! I wish you'd get lost!"

Suddenly the book twisted and turned and rose up in the air. Its bookmark curled like a silky tongue around Steve's head. It licked Steve's right ear. Then it swallowed hard, snapping itself shut.

"Where's he gone?" gasped Tom.

The book belched. "You could try page thirty-one..."

Tom counted through the pages until he found page thirty-one.

There was a picture of a boy and he
looked just like Steve. The boy was lost
in a dark forest. Huge trees with evil
faces twisted and writhed and plucked
at his hair. The boy looked terrified.

"Wish him out if you like," said the book, yawning. "After all, you wished him in."

Tom gulped. "Did I really do that?"

Francesca came over. "Who are you talking to?" she asked.

"No one," said Tom.

"Then you must be bananas!" decided Francesca.

26

Chapter Five

It went on raining after lunch. Miss
Taylor sighed. "I wish it would stop."

"So do I," said Tom. And instantly the
sun came glittering through the
classroom windows.

Oh, no, Tom thought. Not another
wish gone.

"But you don't believe in wishes," teased the book.

"Oh, shut up," whispered Tom.

"I already have," sniffed the book.

Miss Taylor was checking the register.

"Anyone seen Steve Morris?" she asked suddenly. "He was here this morning." She sighed. "That boy is more trouble than a barrel-load of monkeys!"

They went out for afternoon play. The sun was still shining.

28

Tom began to feel awful. Was Steve trapped forever?

"How many wishes can I have?" he asked the book.

"Three, of course," it said. "Says so right here." It opened itself. "Look. And you've had two already..."

"I know, I know." But Tom was thinking hard. "Can I have my third wish now?"

The book waved its silky bookmark. "It's your last one," it sang. "So make it a good one!"

Chapter Six

Tom closed his eyes tightly and crossed his fingers.

"I wish," he said, "for a whole load of new wishes."

"You can't do that!" gasped the book, fluttering its pages.

"But I just have," said Tom, grinning.

He sat down on the bench. "And here comes the next one. I wish Steve Morris wasn't lost."

And there stood Steve, blinking and rubbing his eyes.

Tom turned to the picture on page thirty-one. The boy in the forest wasn't a bit like Steve. He held out the page.

"Want to see?"

But Steve backed off.

Then Miss Taylor spotted him. "Stephen Morris, where have you been?"

"Don't know," sulked Steve. "Got lost, didn't I?"

It worked, thought Tom. Wishes. And lots of them. Wow!

He tried out one of his extra ones.

"Cheating," muttered the book. "No good will come of it!"

But Tom didn't care. "I wish I had an ice cream," he thought, and there it was in his hand.

Francesca watched him unpeeling the silver wrapper.

"Give us a bite," she pleaded.

"OK, just one," said Tom.

"Don't drip it all over my cover," grumbled the book.

Chapter Seven

Back in the sun-filled classroom, Tom
thought of all the things he could wish
for: a puppy, a computer, a new bike...

And when he ran out of wishes, he
could always wish for more.

Suddenly he remembered Mum and
her lost earring.

"I wish she'd find it," he thought. Then he added, "Oooh, and I wish my house was filled with ten pound notes!"

"Oh dear," said the book. "You should have read my next story before making that wish – the one called *How the Sea Came to be Salt*."

But Tom already knew that story, because Miss Taylor had read it. It was about a greedy miller who made a stupid wish.

The miller wished his salt mill would never stop grinding, so that he could get richer and richer and richer. So the mill went on grinding and grinding until everything was covered in great mountains of salt.

Suddenly Tom saw the house filling up with ten pound notes. They oozed out of

the fridge. They covered up the TV. They were piled over the gerbil cage. They filled up the bunk beds and they pushed against the walls. They rose above Mum's face and she began to flap her arms and gasp for air...

Tom panicked.

"I wish I hadn't wished for that," he thought.

Chapter Eight

The minute school was over, Tom ran outside.

He raced up the hill and back down to his street. He belted up the garden path and pressed heavily on the bell.

Mum opened the door. "I'm not deaf," she told him. "What's the big panic?"

Tom felt a bit silly. "Oh, you're ok," he said. "Erm… I was just hungry." Mum sighed and reached for the cake tin. Suddenly she sat down, shaking her head.

"I don't believe it!" she said, pulling out her earring. "It must have come loose when I was putting away the fairy cakes."

Tom grinned. "So I made you find it."

"I suppose you did, love," Mum said.

Then Tom wished that Mum had a big bunch of red roses. He waited and watched, but nothing happened.

Edward came home. "How's your talking book?" he teased.

"Guess what?" said Mum proudly. She pointed at the cake tin. "Tom helped me find my earring!"

"It didn't work," Tom told the book in bed that night.

"You broke the rules," the book whispered. "You cheated. I told you. Those extra wishes simply had to stop before it got out of control."

"Sorry," said Tom.

The book ruffled its pages. "Anyway,

I've got another story..."

"Will you tell it?" asked Tom.

"Maybe..." The book snapped shut. "Or maybe not..."

"Oh, please?" begged Tom.

The book slowly opened and Tom's finger moved along the lines. "Once," the story read, "there was a witch..."

Tom was puzzled. "What's wrong with your voice?" he asked. "It's gone funny."

The book sighed. "That's because it's popped inside your head. It's not *my* voice anymore – it's yours. You're reading. Now put your finger back on the line and stop spoiling the story."

"Wow!" said Tom. "You mean I'm reading on my own?" A shiver went down his back. "I can do it! I can do it!"

And he carried on with the story...

If you enjoyed this story, why not read another *Skylarks* book?

Ghost Mouse
by Karen Wallace and Beccy Blake

When the new owners of Honeycomb Cottage move in, the mice that live there are not happy. They like the cottage just as it is and Melanie and Hugo have plans to change everything. But the mice of Honeycomb Cottage are no ordinary mice. They set out to scare Melanie and Hugo away. They *are* ghost mice after all, and isn't that what ghosts do best?

Yasmin's Parcels

by Jill Atkins and Lauren Tobia

Yasmin lives in a tiny house with her mama and papa and six little brothers and sisters. They are poor and hungry and, as the oldest child, Yasmin knows she needs to do something to help. So, she sets off to find some food. But Yasmin can't find any food and, instead, is given some mysterious parcels. How can these parcels help her feed her family?

45

Muffin

by Anne Rooney and Sean Julian

One day, Caitlin finds a baby bird sitting in a broken eggshell. She takes the bird home to the lighthouse and decides to call him Muffin. Muffin is very happy being fed tasty slivers of fish and sleeping in the cosy sock Caitlin has given him, but the time comes when every baby bird must learn to look after itself and Caitlin has to set Muffin free....

The Black Knight

by Mick Gowar and Graham Howells

One dark night, a mysterious stranger
visited *The Green Man* inn. He told the
tale of a magnificent treasure, which
had been buried nearby in the time of
King Arthur. This treasure was
protected by the Black Knight. The men
in the inn wanted the treasure but they
were all too afraid to challenge the
fearsome knight. Tom, the innkeeper's
nephew, had other ideas….

Skylarks titles include:

Awkward Annie
by Julia Williams and Tim Archbold
HB 9780237533847
PB 9780237534028

Sleeping Beauty
by Louise John and Natascia Ugliano
HB 9780237533861
PB 9780237534042

Detective Derek
by Karen Wallace and Beccy Blake
HB 9780237533885
PB 9780237534066

Hurricane Season
by David Orme and Doreen Lang
HB 9780237533892
PB 9780237534073

Spiggy Red
by Penny Dolan and Cinzia Battistel
HB 9780237533854
PB 9780237534035

London's Burning
by Pauline Francis and Alessandro
Baldanzi
HB 9780237533878
PB 9780237534059

The Black Knight
by Mick Gowar and Graham Howells
HB 9780237535803
PB 9780237535926

Ghost Mouse
by Karen Wallace and Beccy Blake
HB 9780237535827
PB 9780237535940

Yasmin's Parcels
by Jill Atkins and Lauren Tobia
HB 9780237535858
PB 9780237535971

Muffin
by Anne Rooney and Sean Julian
HB 9780237535810
PB 9780237535933

Tallulah and the Tea Leaves
by Louise John and Vian Oelofsen
HB 9780237535841
PB 9780237535964

The Big Purple Wonderbook
by Enid Richemont and Kelly Waldek
HB 9780237535834
PB 9780237535957